P9-CEB-234

PINKY and REX and the New Baby

PINKY and REX
and the
New Baby

by James Howe
illustrated by Melissa Sweet

SCHOLASTIC INC.

New York Toronto London Auckland Sydney
Mexico City New Delhi Hong Kong

No part of this publication may be reproduced in whole or in part, or stored in a retrieval system, or transmitted in any form or by any means, electronic, mechanical, photocopying, recording, or otherwise, without written permission of the publisher.
For information regarding permission, write to Atheneum Books for Young Readers, Simon & Schuster Children's Publishing Division, 1230 Avenue of the Americas, New York, NY 10020.

ISBN 0-439-11478-0

Text copyright © 1993 by James Howe. Illustrations copyright © 1993 by Melissa Sweet. All rights reserved. Published by Scholastic Inc., 555 Broadway, New York, NY 10012 by arrangement with Atheneum Books for Young Readers, Simon & Schuster Children's Publishing Division. SCHOLASTIC and associated logos are trademarks and/or registered trademarks of Scholastic Inc.

12 11 10 9 8 7 6 5 4   1 2 3 4/0

Printed in the U.S.A.   09

First Scholastic printing, November 1999

The text of this book was set in Utopia.
The illustrations were rendered in watercolor.

For Helise, Sy, Adam & Lauren,
and
for Joanna, Don & Ari
—J. H.

For Lenny
—M. S.

Contents

Chapter 1
The Invisible Girl

Rex couldn't believe it. "We're going to have a *what*?" she asked.

"A baby," her mother answered with a big smile. "Isn't it wonderful?"

Her father was smiling, too. "You know we've been talking about this for a long time now, Rex. Well, it's finally going to happen. What do you think?"

Rex shrugged. "It's okay," she
said. "Can I go over to Pinky's house?"
    Her mother's smile faded. "But,
Rex—"
    "That's all right," said Rex's
father. "We can talk more about it
another time. You go ahead, Rex."
    Rex ran out of the house as fast
as she could. By the time she reached

Pinky's house across the street, her cheeks were burning.

"What's wrong?" Pinky asked as soon as he saw her.

"We're going to have a *baby*," Rex said, almost spitting the word.

"But that's neat, Rex," Pinky said. "It'll be fun having a baby around."

"I don't *want* to have a baby around," said Rex, plopping herself down on the front step. Pinky sat down next to her.

Rex was surprised that Pinky didn't understand. He was her best friend. And besides, he had a pesky little sister. Wasn't he always telling Rex how lucky she was to be an only child?

"I like things the way they are,"
Rex said. "Just me and my mom and
dad. Now they'll spend all their time
with the baby. I'll bet they won't
even know I'm around."

4

"Sure they will," said Pinky.

"Uh-uh. I'll be the invisible girl."

Pinky tried not to laugh, but he couldn't help himself. "Don't be dopey. Hey, you want to help me put together my new model?"

Rex shook her head.

"Want to go for a ride on our bikes?"

Rex shook her head again.

"How about a game of soccer?"

Rex looked up. "Do you have a ball?" she asked. Soccer was her new favorite sport.

"Well, not a real soccer ball, but—"

"Then forget it," said Rex, resting her chin in her hands. "I don't want to play, anyway."

"What *do* you want to do?"
"I don't know. Yes, I do."
"What?" Pinky asked.
Rex started to tell him, then wondered if he'd understand. "Oh, nothing," she said. But she was already thinking about it. She was going to come up with a plan to make sure she didn't turn into the Invisible Girl.

Chapter 2
Meeting Matthew

A few days later Pinky watched from his bedroom window as the car pulled into the driveway of the house across the street.

"They're home!" he shouted.

His little sister, Amanda, ran into the room, clutching a pink dinosaur dressed in a diaper and bib. "I was

just feeding Poopsie," she announced,
squeezing in beside her brother at
the window. "Let *me* see. Ooo, look,
there it is!"

"It's not an 'it,' it's a 'he,'" said

8

Pinky. "Mom says his name is Matthew."

"Ooo, he's so cute!" Amanda squealed.

"You can't see his face from here," Pinky said. "He's all wrapped up."

Amanda shook her head at Pinky. "He's a baby," she explained. "*All* babies are cute, don't you know that?" She shoved the pink dinosaur into his face. "Don't you think Poopsie is cute?"

Pinky groaned.

Suddenly he heard his name being called. He looked out the window again and saw Rex waving to him from across the street. She looked happy.

"Come on over!" Rex shouted.

Moments later Pinky's entire
family had gathered across the street
to greet their neighbors and meet the
little bundle in Rex's mother's arms.

"Can I hold him, Mom?" Rex
was saying when they got there.

"In a minute," her mother said.
She was opening the blanket so Pinky
and his family could all get a look.

"Ooo, he's so cute!" Amanda

cried. She held the dinosaur high up in the air. "Look, Poopsie, a new little friend. You two can play together."

Pinky had never imagined anyone's face could be so tiny. "He *is* kinda cute," he said to Rex. "In a squinched-up sort of way."

"*All* babies look like that at first," Rex said in the voice of an expert. "Please, Mom, let me hold him."

"All right," said her mother. She handed the baby to Rex, who took him very carefully.

"She's good with him," Pinky's mother commented.

"Oh, yes, Rex is going to be a wonderful big sister," said Rex's mother.

"She already *is* a wonderful big sister," said Rex's father.

Rex beamed. Her plan was working perfectly.

Chapter 3
Where Did the Baby Come From?

That night at dinner, Pinky asked, "Is Rex adopted?"

"No," said his mother.

"But Matthew is."

"That's true," Pinky's mother said. She noticed Amanda slipping some string beans into the napkin on her lap. "Try eating them," she suggested.

Amanda looked surprised. "What? Oh, I *was* going to eat them. I was just, um, saving them for later. For a treat."

"Right," said Pinky. "Nothing like a few cold string beans while you watch TV."

Amanda glared at Pinky and dumped the string beans back on her plate.

"Where did the baby come from, anyway?" Pinky asked.

"Well, it's like this," Pinky's father said, drawing out the words. Pinky knew they were now on an Important Subject and his father was trying to find just the right thing to say.

"Are we adopted?" Amanda asked. She made a great show of

slowly and noisily sucking a string
bean into her mouth.

Her father shook his head. "No.
Your mother gave birth to both of
you. And Rex's mother gave birth to
her. But when Rex's parents wanted
to have a second child, they found
they couldn't."

"Why?" Pinky asked.

Pinky's father shrugged. "It just happens sometimes and no one knows why."

"Then who did give birth to Matthew?" Amanda asked.

"Matthew's birth mother is a young woman who loved him very much," said their mother. "But she realized she simply couldn't take care of him."

"Why not?" asked Amanda.

"I don't know enough about her to tell you that," her mother said. "Perhaps she was very poor and already had children. Maybe she was young and knew that Matthew needed someone older to be a good mother to him. I do know this: She loved him so much that she was willing to let other people become his parents. She knew that that would be best for him."

Pinky nodded thoughtfully. "You know what I don't get?" he asked. "I don't get why Rex is acting so weird. First she didn't even want this baby and now she's so happy about it."

"Maybe her feelings changed when she actually met him," his

mother answered. "You were just the opposite when Amanda was born. You could hardly wait for the baby to come and then when we brought her home, you took one look at her, marched up to your room, packed a bag, and told us you were moving to Disney World."

Pinky turned and looked at his sister, who had two string-bean fangs hanging out of her mouth.

"Is that bag still packed?" he asked.

Chapter 4
"I'm the Big Sister!"

The next day Rex's two grandmothers and two grandfathers came to visit. Each set of grandparents gave her a T-shirt that read I'M THE BIG SISTER! Her mother and father had already bought her a similar one before they'd gone to get Matthew, so now she had three. In order to avoid hurting anyone's feelings, she planned to wear one in the morning, a different one in the afternoon, and the third one in the evening.

"So I guess you feel pretty good about having a baby brother, after all," Pinky said to Rex late that afternoon. Rex had just put on the third T-shirt and was changing Matthew's diaper.

She nodded happily. "Mom says she never knew I could be such a big help. She's let me feed Matthew all by myself *four* times. I even taught my grandpa Charles how to burp him. He said he'd never even burped his own babies."

"Oh," said Pinky, not sure what else to say. "Do you want to go out and play when you're finished?"

"Can't," said Rex. "Once Matthew goes down for his nap, I promised Mom I would help her start planning for the party on Saturday." She turned her attention back to the baby.

Pinky frowned, but Rex didn't even notice. She was too busy singing, "The itsy-bitsy spider went up the waterspout..."

Chapter 5
The Party

When Rex's family had the welcome-home party for Matthew the following Saturday, it was the first time in a week Rex wasn't wearing a T-shirt that read I'M THE BIG SISTER! Instead she wore a sweatshirt that read #1 BIG SISTER!

"Where'd you get *that*?" Pinky asked in a tone Amanda would have called "snotty" if she'd heard him.

"From my aunt Susan," Rex said.

Pinky noticed that she had a cloth diaper draped over her shoulder. "What's that there for?" he asked.

"In case the baby spits up, silly," Rex answered matter-of-factly.

"But you're not holding the baby," said Pinky.

"No, but I like to have it there just in case."

Pinky didn't wait around to find out in case of what. He rolled his eyes and headed for the punch bowl. What was going on, anyway? Rex just wasn't her same old self anymore. She never wanted to play with him. She never wanted to do anything but take care of the baby.

For the next hour or so, Pinky

and Amanda played with some of Rex's cousins. From time to time, Pinky checked to see what Rex was doing. She was always either holding Matthew or sitting next to whoever else was holding Matthew or running to get Matthew a bottle or pacifier or blanket or toy. Once, Pinky motioned for her to join him and

some of the other kids. For a
moment it looked as if she would.
But then she just shook her head.

"The game is starting," he heard
someone say a short time later.

"What game?" Pinky asked Ben,
Rex's nine-year-old cousin.

"World Cup soccer match on
TV," Ben said. "Want to watch?"

Pinky shrugged. He wasn't all
that interested in soccer. Rex was,
though.

That's why he couldn't
understand why she didn't join the
others. Instead Rex stayed right
where she was, close to her mother
and Matthew.

Something was definitely wrong.

Chapter 6
The Shopping Trip

"I'm glad I waited to buy a baby gift," Pinky's mother said as she pulled the car into a parking spot. "You wouldn't believe all the things Matthew has already. But I know one thing he doesn't have—a toy chest."

"I know what *I'm* getting him," Amanda piped up as she unbuckled her seat belt. She grabbed Poopsie and jumped out of the car. "A teddy bear!"

"That's what I was going to get!" said Pinky.

Pinky's parents had told both children they could get their own gifts for Matthew.

"Too bad," said Amanda. "Poopsie and I talked about it and that's what we're getting. So you're outvoted. Two to one."

"Mom!"

"Now, look, you two, I don't want any arguing. I know that Amanda has her heart set on a teddy bear, Pinky. Why don't we just let her

get that for Matthew and you can get
another kind of stuffed animal,
okay?"

"Okay," Pinky mumbled. He
knew his mother was expecting him
to be mature. He hated it when he
had to act like a big brother. Why did
Rex think being a big sister was so
great, anyway?

"Mom," Pinky said as they entered the store, "do you think Rex will ever be normal again?"

His mother smiled, but before she could answer, Amanda said, "Rex is a girl. You're a boy. You don't understand these things. Right, Mom?"

"Being a boy or a girl has nothing to do with it, Amanda."

"Oh."

Pinky's mother turned to him. "You miss Rex, don't you?" she asked. Pinky nodded. "Well, I think she misses you, too."

"Really?"

"Really. I think Rex is trying very hard to be a perfect big sister right now. She wants to be sure her parents don't forget about her. I know it's hard, but try to be patient. She'll be back to normal soon."

Suddenly Pinky spotted something. "Mom," he said, "can I buy a present for Rex, too?"

"I think that would be nice," said his mother. Then seeing what was hanging on the rack in front of them, she said, "I don't think she needs another 'Big Sister' T-shirt."

"That's not it," Pinky said. He reached for what he wanted to get her.

His mother nodded. "She'll love it," she said.

Chapter 7
Back to Normal

Rex did love it. "Wow, a dinosaur T-shirt! And I don't have one like it, Pinky. Where'd you find it?"

"The same place I got this," he said.

He handed her his present for
Matthew. It was the last gift to be
opened. While Pinky's family
watched, Rex's mother had
unwrapped the toy chest. Her father
had unwrapped the teddy bear from
Amanda. Now it was Rex's turn.

"A soccer ball?" she asked. "But
Matthew's too little for a soccer ball."

"I know," said Pinky. "I figured Matthew would like to have a soccer ball that's been broken in for him. You know, like the catcher's mitt you said you're going to give him someday."

Rex rolled the ball around in her hands. "It's a beauty," she said. "Just like the pros use."

Just then Matthew, who was lying in his carriage nearby, began to cry. Rex jumped up, but her mother stopped her.

"I'll get him," she said, putting down her tea. "Why don't you go out and play for a little while? There's still some daylight left."

Rex gave the soccer ball a loving look. "Well, if you're sure it's okay."

As Rex's mother picked Matthew up and propped him on her shoulder, she said, "You've been terrific with the baby, but go out and have some fun. Before you know it, Matthew will be trailing around after you and you'll be complaining that he's a pain in the neck."

"I'll never think he's a pain in the neck," said Rex.

Pinky poked Rex and nodded toward Amanda, who was tickling Poopsie under his chin and making little goo-goo noises. Rex looked long and hard at Amanda.

"Maybe Pinky and I *will* go out to play," she said. She tossed Pinky the soccer ball and put on her new T-shirt.

Amanda jumped up. "Wait for me!" she shouted.

"No way," Pinky and Rex cried out together.

Amanda's eyes flared. "Mom! Dad!"

"I think they'd like to play by themselves right now, Amanda," said

her father. "Why don't you stay in here with us? We know how much you like babies. Maybe you can spend a little time with Matthew."

Amanda dropped Poopsie to the floor and crossed her arms. "Not fair!" she said, sticking out her lower lip.

Moments later Pinky and Rex were kicking the soccer ball around the front yard. "Watch this!" Rex cried. She tossed the ball in the air and bounced it off her head. "Neat, huh?"

Pinky smiled. Rex was back to normal at last.